PHONICS

Book 1
Short A

Give It Back!

SCHOLASTIC

Give It Back!

Note to parents:
Pokémon names can be hard to pronounce!
Please use this guide to help your child sound
out the names included in this book:

Pikachu: PEE-ka-choo

Sandile: SAN-dyle

Ducklett: DUK-lit

by Quinlan B. Lee

Published by Scholastic Inc., *Publishers since 1920.* SCHOLASTIC and associated logos are trademarks and/or registered trademarks of Scholastic Inc.

The publisher does not have any control over and does not assume any responsibility for author or third-party websites or their content.

Scholastic Inc., 557 Broadway, New York, NY 10012

978-1-338-23094-9

10 9 8 7 6 5 4   21 22 23 24 25

Printed in Ruwang, Malaysia   106
First printing 2018

SCHOLASTIC INC.

Pikachu and Sandile are in a **battle**. Ducklett cuts into the **match**.

Ducklett **grabs** Sandile's **glasses**.
It will not give them **back**.

Sandile is **sad**.
"Let's get your **glasses back**,"
says Ash.

Ducklett **grabs** Ash's **hat**.
"Give **back** my **hat**!" Ash yells.

Now Ash is **mad**.
He **grabs** Sandile.
"Let's **battle**!" he says.

Ash sees three Ducklett.
One has the **glasses**.
One has his **hat**.

Pikachu **zaps** one Ducklett.
It **blasts back at** Pikachu.

One Ducklett **attacks** Ash.
It **traps** him in ice.
Now Ash is very **mad**!

Sandile **cracks** the ice.

"Thanks," says Ash.

"Let's get **that hat** and **glasses**."

Sandile is **mad.**
It is ready to **battle.**
"ATTACK!" says Ash.

Sandile **attacks**.
The three Ducklett **blast back**.

Pikachu blocks the **attacks**.
But the Ducklett use more
attacks!

Now Pikachu is **mad**.
It **blasts back** a big **attack**.

At last, the Ducklett fly away.
"You did it!" Ash tells Pikachu.
"The Ducklett will not be **back**."

They got the **hat** and
glasses back!

Ducklett **grabs** Sandile's **glasses**.
Can Ash and Pikachu get them **back**?

In this book, you will practice these **short A** words:

back	at	attack
grab	battle	blast
mad	crack	glasses
sad	hat	last
zap	match	pan
	that	trap

978-1-338-23094-9

scholastic.com

PHONICS

Book 2
Short E

Get the Egg!

Note to parents:

Pokémon names can be hard to pronounce!
Please use this guide to help your child sound
out the names included in this book:

Totodile: TOE-toe-dyle

Cyndaquil: SIN-da-kwill

by Quinlan B. Lee

© 2018 The Pokémon Company International. © 1997–2018 Nintendo, Creatures, GAME FREAK, TV Tokyo,
ShoPro, JR Kikaku. TM, ® Nintendo.

Published by Scholastic Inc., *Publishers since 1920.* SCHOLASTIC and associated logos are trademarks
and/or registered trademarks of Scholastic Inc.

Scholastic Inc., 557 Broadway, New York, NY 10012

978-1-338-23095-6

10 9 8 7 6 5 4   21 22 23 24 25

Printed in Rawang, Malaysia   106
First printing 2018

SCHOLASTIC INC.

Dawn wins a prize.

She **gets** an **Egg**.

Team Rocket **jets** by.
Now they **get** the **Egg**!

Team Rocket almost
gets away.
But they hit a **nest**.

Dawn and her friends see
Team Rocket crash.
"**Help**!" Jessie **yells**.

They run to the **nest**.
Dawn wants to **get** her
Egg back.

Dawn **gets** to James.
She wants to **get** the **Egg**.
"**Help**!" James **yells**.

His Pokémon wants to **help**.
It bites his head.

Totodile **jets** by.
It **gets** the **Egg**.

Dawn **gets** the **Egg** back.
The **shell** glows.

What **gets** out of the **shell**?
It is Cyndaquil!

Its back fires up!
Dawn **gets** very hot!

Dawn is glad.
She **gets** a new friend!

Dawn **gets** an **Egg**.
Team Rocket takes it!
Can Dawn **get** the **Egg** back?

In this book, you will practice these **short E** words:

Egg	get	help
jet	nest	shell
yell		

978-1-338-23095-6

scholastic.com

Get Your Licks!

Note to parents:

Pokémon names can be hard to pronounce!
Please use this guide to help your child sound
out the names included in this book:

Lickilicky: LICK-ee-LICK-ee

Pikachu: PEE-ka-choo

Piplup: PIP-plup

Shinx: SHINKS

by Quinlan B. Lee

© 2018 The Pokémon Company International. © 1997–2018 Nintendo, Creatures, GAME FREAK, TV Tokyo, ShoPro, JR Kikaku. TM, ® Nintendo.

Published by Scholastic Inc., *Publishers since 1920.* SCHOLASTIC and associated logos are trademarks and/or registered trademarks of Scholastic Inc.

The publisher does not have any control over and does not assume any responsibility for author or third-party websites or their content.

Scholastic Inc., 557 Broadway, New York, NY 10012

978-1-338-23097-0

10 9 8 7 6 5 4   21 22 23 24 25

Printed in Rawang, Malaysia   106
First printing 2018

SCHOLASTIC INC.

Angie takes care of Lickilicky.
Lickilicky **is big**.
It is pink.

Lickilicky does not like **its** Poké Ball.
So Angie **hid it in** a cave.

Lickilicky naps **in its** cave.
It gets a **whiff** of food.

It licks the Poké food.
It licks with its big pink tongue.

It is a **trick**!
Team Rocket wants to
get Lickilicky.

Ash sees the **trick**.
But **it is** too late.

It is not too late for Pikachu.
It zips into battle **with** Shinx
and Piplup.

Pikachu **zips** to Team Rocket.
It hits them **with** a bolt.

Team Rocket **flips** up **in** the air.
The **trick is** over!

Now the **big pink**
Pokémon **is** safe.

Team Rocket **tricks** Lickilicky.
Pikachu **zips** to help the **big pink**
Pokémon.

In this book, you will practice these **short I** words:

big	flip	give
grin	hid	him
hit	in	is
it	its	lick
pink	trick	whiff
with	zip	

978-1-338-23097-0

PHONICS

Stop That Shot!

SCHOLASTIC

Book 4
Short O

Stop That Shot!

Note to parents:
Pokémon names can be hard to pronounce!
Please use this guide to help your child sound
out the names included in this book:

Emolga: ee-MAHL-guh
Simisear: SIH-mee-seer
Snivy: SNY-vee

by Quinlan B. Lee

© 2018 The Pokémon Company International. © 1997–2018 Nintendo, Creatures, GAME FREAK, TV Tokyo, ShoPro, JR Kikaku. TM, ® Nintendo.

Published by Scholastic Inc., *Publishers since 1920.* SCHOLASTIC and associated logos are trademarks and/or registered trademarks of Scholastic Inc.

Scholastic Inc., 557 Broadway, New York, NY 10012

978-1-338-23098-7

10 9 8 7 6 5 4   21 22 23 24 25

Printed in Rawang, Malaysia   106
First printing 2018

SCHOLASTIC INC.

Emolga eats a **lot** of fruit.
It does **not stop**.
It does **not** share.

Emolga **tosses** a core.
STOP!

But it is too late.
The core hits Simisear.
Simisear is **not** happy.

Stomp, stomp, stomp!
Simisear is **hot**!

Emolga does **not** care.
It **hops** away.

Simisear takes a **shot** at Emolga.
Snivy must **stop** the **shot**.

Simisear takes one more **shot**.
Snivy can **not stop** it.

Emolga has to **stop** it.
It **hops** into battle.

But it does **not** hit Simisear.
The **shot** hits a big **rock**.

The **rock** will **drop**.
It will **drop** on **top** of Simisear!
Who can **stop** the **rock**?

Emolga and Snivy **stop** the **rock**.
They blast the **rock**.

"Good **job**!" Iris says.

"Good **shot**!" Ash says.

Now Emolga shares **lots** of fruit.
It has **lots** of friends!

Emolga eats a **lot**.
It does **not** share.
Stop, Emolga!

In this book, you will practice these **short O** words:

drop	hop	hot
job	lot	not
rock	shot	stomp
stop	top	· toss

978-1-338-23098-7

scholastic.com

PHONICS

Run Away

Book 5
Short U

Run Away

Note to parents:
Pokémon names can be hard to pronounce!
Please use this guide to help your child sound
out the names included in this book:

Gible: GIB-bull

Piplup: PIP-plup

Pikachu: PEE-ka-choo

by Quinlan B. Lee

Published by Scholastic Inc., *Publishers since 1920.* SCHOLASTIC and associated logos are trademarks and/or registered trademarks of Scholastic Inc.

The publisher does not have any control over and does not assume any responsibility for author or third-party websites or their content.

Scholastic Inc., 557 Broadway, New York, NY 10012

978-1-338-23100-7

10 9 8 7 6 5 4   21 22 23 24 25

Printed in Rawang, Malaysia   106
First printing 2018

SCHOLASTIC INC.

Gible shoots an attack.
It goes **up**, **up**, **up**.

The attack comes down
with a **thud**.
It **bumps** Piplup.
Ow!

Gible **jumps** on Piplup.
That is too **much**!

Piplup **bumps** Gible **up, up, up.**
Gible comes down with a **thud.**
It **bumps** its head.

Ash, Dawn, and Brock **run** to Gible.
They **rub** the **bump** on its head.

No one **runs** to Piplup.
No one **rubs** the **bump** on
its head.
Piplup **runs** away.

Piplup **runs** into new pals.
It tells them about its **bump**.

Dawn **jumps up**.
She **must** find Piplup.
She **runs** into the woods.

Pikachu **bumps** into Piplup.
Pikachu **must run** to get Dawn.

Piplup wants to **run** to its new pals.
But…

They are not new pals.
They are Team Rocket!
They lock **up** the Pokémon!

Ash and Dawn **run up**.
They free the Pokémon.
Dawn **hugs** Piplup.

Piplup is mad at Team Rocket.
It uses a new **pump** move.

The **pump bumps** Team
Rocket.
They go **up**, **up**, **up** in the air.

Dawn **hugs** Piplup.
"Never **run** away again,"
she says.
"*Piplup!*" it says.

Gible **jumps** on Piplup.
Thud! That is too **much**.
Piplup **runs** away.

In this book, you will practice these **short U** words:

bump	but	hug
jump	much	must
pump	rub	run
thud	up	

978-1-338-23100-7

PHONICS

Book 6
Short Vowel
Review

Catch Z2!

SCHOLASTIC

Catch Z2!

by Quinlan B. Lee

© 2018 The Pokémon Company International. © 1997–2018 Nintendo, Creatures, GAME FREAK, TV Tokyo, ShoPro, JR Kikaku. TM, ® Nintendo.

Published by Scholastic Inc., *Publishers since 1920.* SCHOLASTIC and associated logos are trademarks and/or registered trademarks of Scholastic Inc.

Scholastic Inc., 557 Broadway, New York, NY 10012

978-1-338-23101-4

10 9 8 7 6 5 4   21 22 23 24 25

Printed in Rawang, Malaysia   106
First printing 2018

SCHOLASTIC INC.

Bonnie gives her **new** Pokémon a **kiss**.
She and Squishy are **best** friends.

Does Squishy need a **nap**?
No. **But** Squishy is **sad**.

Squishy is **sad**.
Its friend, Z2, needs **help**.

Z2 does need **help**!
It is in a **trap**.

Team Flare wants to **catch it**.

Who **can help** Z2?

Z2 **jumps up**.
It calls for **help**!
Cells come to **help**.
They form a Zygarde.

Zygarde **can help**!
It ducks the **blasts**.

Zygarde **runs**.
It turns **back** into Z2.

Team Rocket **traps** Z2.
They **grab it** and **run**.

Team Rocket hides by a **rock**.
Now Z2 is **sad**.

James **thinks** Z2 needs a **nap**.

"**It** does **not** need a **nap**," says Jessie. "**It** needs **help**."

Team Rocket **can help** Z2.

Z2 is **sad**.
It needs **help**!
Can Team Rocket **help** it?

In this book, you will practice these **short vowel** words:

back	best	can
blast	but	duck
catch	cell	it
grab	help	kiss
its	jump	not
nap	new	sad
rock	run	trap
up	think	

978-1-338-23101-4

scholastic.com

PHONICS

Save the Day

PHONICS

Book 7
Long A

Save the Day

Note to parents:

Pokémon names can be hard to pronounce! Please use this guide to help your child sound out the names included in this book:

Zebstrika: zehb-STRY-kuh

Palpitoad: PAL-pih-tohd

Emolga: ee-MAHL-guh

Snivy: SNY-vee

Pikachu: PEE-ka-cho

by Quinlan B. Lee

Published by Scholastic Inc., *Publishers since 1920.* SCHOLASTIC and associated logos are trademarks and/or registered trademarks of Scholastic Inc.

The publisher does not have any control over and does not assume any responsibility for author or third-party websites or their content.

Scholastic Inc., 557 Broadway, New York, NY 10012

978-1-338-23124-3

10 9 8 7 6 5 4   21 22 23 24 25

Printed in Rawang, Malaysia   106
First printing 2018

SCHOLASTIC INC.

Ash **takes** on Elesa.
"**Game** on!" he says.
He wants to win a Gym badge.

Elesa's Zebstrika **races** out.
Ash's Palpitoad **chases** it.

Zebstrika **flames** up.
But Palpitoad does not **shake**.

Palpitoad is a Water-type.
Flames do not **make** it **shake**.

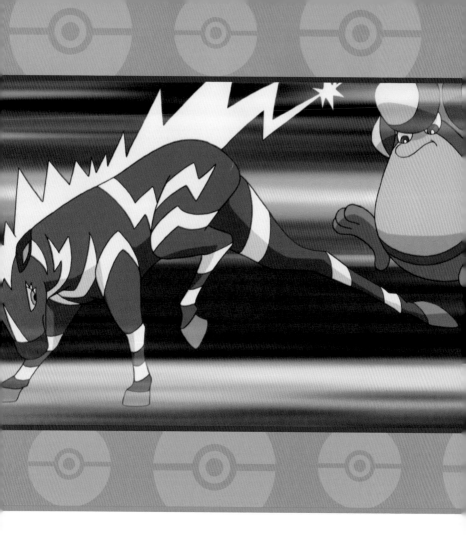

Palpitoad **chases** Zebstrika.
Zebstrika kicks it.
Palpitoad is in a **daze**.

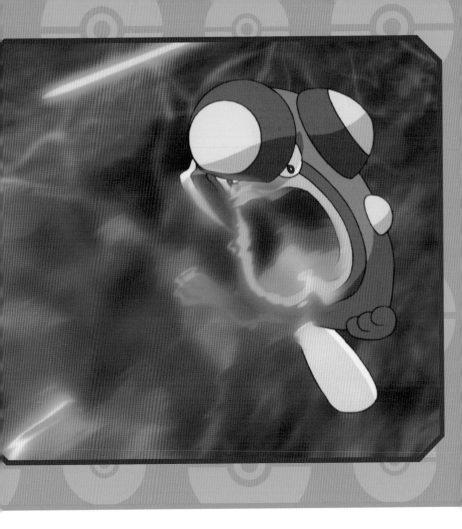

Palpitoad **makes** its move.
It blasts Zebstrika!

Zebstrika cannot **take** the blast.
It is in a **daze**.
Palpitoad wins!

Elesa's Emolga **takes** on Palpitoad.
Emolga is a flying **ace**.

Emolga **makes** its move.
It puts Palpitoad in a love **daze**.

The **ace** flies in.
Who can **save** Palpitoad?

Snivy **saves** the **day**!
It **takes** on Emolga.
But Emolga flies **away**.

Ash needs Pikachu.
Pikachu will **save** the **day**.

Pikachu **takes** on Emolga.
They blast with the **same** move.
Pikachu **saves** the match!

Hooray!
Ash wins his badge.
It is a good **day**!

Game on!
Ash wants to win a Gym badge.
Can Pikachu **take** on Emolga?

In this book, you will practice these **long A** words:

ace	away	chase
day	daze	flame
game	hooray	same
make	race	take
save	shake	

978-1-338-23124-3

scholastic.com

PHONICS

Book 8
Long E

The Three Brothers

SCHOLASTIC

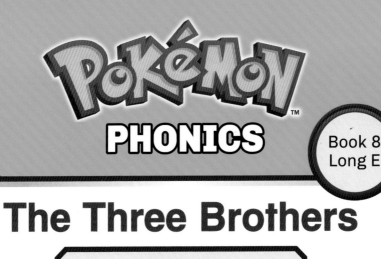

The Three Brothers

Note to parents:
Pokémon names can be hard to pronounce!
Please use this guide to help your child sound
out the names included in this book:

Pikachu: PEE-ka-choo
Pansage: PAN-sayj
Panpour: PAN-por
Pansear: PAN-seer

by Quinlan B. Lee

© 2018 The Pokémon Company International. © 1997–2018 Nintendo, Creatures, GAME FREAK, TV Tokyo, ShoPro, JR Kikaku. TM, ® Nintendo.

Published by Scholastic Inc., *Publishers since 1920.* SCHOLASTIC and associated logos are trademarks and/or registered trademarks of Scholastic Inc.

Scholastic Inc., 557 Broadway, New York, NY 10012

978-1-338-23125-0

10 9 8 7 6 5 4   21 22 23 24 25

Printed in Rawang, Malaysia   106
First printing 2018

SCHOLASTIC INC.

Ash and Pikachu look up
the **street**.
They try to **see** the Gym.

They **meet** a boy in the **street**.
He has **green** hair.
"Do you **see** the Gym?" Ash asks.

The boy brings Ash to the Gym.
Ash **meets** the Gym **Leaders**.

It does not **seem** like a Gym.
It **seems** like a place to **eat**.

Three boys **greet** them.
"Who **leads** this Gym?"
asks Ash.

Three brothers **lead** the Gym.
"**Three** Gym **Leaders**?!" Ash says.

One is the boy with the
green hair, Cilan.

Ash **meets** his
Pokémon, Pansage.

Ash **meets** Cress.
He meets his Pokémon,
Panpour.

Ash **meets** Chili.
He meets his Pokémon,
Pansear.

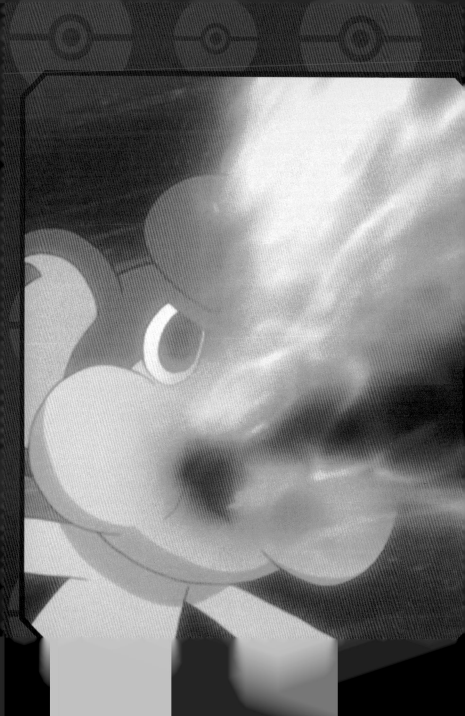

Pansear brings the **heat**.
Ash has to **beat** that
heat!

Ash wants to win the Gym badge.
He must **beat these** Pokémon in **three** matches.

Can Ash do it?
Wait and **see**!

Ash **meets three** Gym **Leaders**.
He wants to **beat** them!
Can Ash take the **heat**?

In this book, you will practice these **long E** words:

beat	eat	green
greet	he	heat
lead	Leader	seem
meet	see	three
street	these	

978-1-338-23125-0

scholastic.com

PHONICS

Book 9
Long I

Time to Battle

PHONICS

**Book 9
Long I**

Time to Battle

Note to parents:

Pokémon names can be hard to pronounce! Please use this guide
to help your child sound out the names included in this book:

Tepig: TEH-pig
Pansear: PAN-seer
Pikachu: PEE-ka-choo
Panpour: PAN-por
Oshawott: AH-shuh-wot
Pansage: PAN-sayj

by Quinlan B. Lee

Published by Scholastic Inc., *Publishers since 1920.* SCHOLASTIC and associated logos are trademarks
and/or registered trademarks of Scholastic Inc.

The publisher does not have any control over and does not assume any responsibility for
author or third-party websites or their content.

Scholastic Inc., 557 Broadway, New York, NY 10012

978-1-338-23127-4

10 9 8 7 6 5 4   21 22 23 24 25

Printed in Rawang, Malaysia   106
First printing 2018

SCHOLASTIC INC.

"**Time** to battle!" Ash **cries**.
First in **line** is Tepig.
It will battle Pansear.

Pansear **tries** to blast Tepig.
Tepig grabs its tail in **time**.
It takes Pansear for a **ride**.

Tepig wins the match.
Ash **smiles**.
"**Nice** move," he says.

Next in **line** is Pikachu.
Pikachu will take on Panpour.

Panpour **swipes** Pikachu.
The Pokémon **flies** through
the air.

Pikachu **wipes** out.

Panpour wins the match.
"**Nice try**," Ash says.

The battle is a **tie**.
Oshawott is last in **line**.
It **tries** to battle Pansage.

Pansage **fires** at Oshawott.
Oshawott **tries** to **fire** back.

It misses.
"*Oshawott . . .*" it **cries**.

Seeds **fly** at Oshawott.
"**Try** to get up!" Ash tells it.
"We are on your **side**."

Oshawott will not **cry**.
It will **try**!

Oshawott **fires** a big blast.
It is a **nice** move.
Panpour **tries** to **hide**.

The blast hits Panpour.
It falls to its **side**.

Oshawott and Ash win the badge!

"Time to battle!" Ash yells.
His Pokémon get in **line**!
Who will **try** first?

In this book, you will practice these **long I** words:

cry	line	fire
fly	side	nice
ride	tie	smile
swipe	wipe	time
try		

978-1-338-23127-4

scholastic.com

PHONICS

Book 10
Long O

Go Home, Pokémon

SCHOLASTIC

Go Home, Pokémon

by Quinlan B. Lee

© 2018 The Pokémon Company International. © 1997–2018 Nintendo, Creatures, GAME FREAK, TV Tokyo, ShoPro, JR Kikaku. TM, ® Nintendo.

Published by Scholastic Inc., *Publishers since 1920.* SCHOLASTIC and associated logos are trademarks and/or registered trademarks of Scholastic Inc.

Scholastic Inc., 557 Broadway, New York, NY 10012

978-1-338-23128-1

10 9 8 7 6 5 4   21 22 23 24 25

Printed in Rawang, Malaysia   106
First printing 2018

SCHOLASTIC INC.

Buizel and Aipom are in a battle.
Wham! Bam!
A blast hits some **stones**.

Oh no!
The **stones glow**.

Smoke blows.
The **glow goes** up into
the sky.

It is Spiritomb!

"The Pokémon **woke** it up," says Dawn.

"They **broke** its **stone home**."

Spiritomb tries to blast Ash
and Pikachu.
It blasts a big **hole**.

"That was **close**!" Ash yells.
"Let's put it back in its **stone home**."

Ash sees **bolts** in the sky.
He **knows** what to do.

Pikachu grabs a **bolt**.
It starts to **glow**.

Pikachu blasts Spiritomb with a big **bolt**.

Spiritomb **goes** back into its **stone home**.

Ash and his friends put back the **stones**.

The **stones glow**.
Spiritomb is back in its
stone home.

"Welcome **home**, Spiritomb,"
Ash says.

Oh no!
Spiritomb **broke** out of its **stone home**.
Can Ash and Pikachu **bolt** it back in?

In this book, you will practice these **long O** words:

blow	bolt	broke
close	go	glow
hole	home	oh
know	no	woke
smoke	stone	

978-1-338-23128-1

PHONICS

Book 11
Long U

Cute Blue Shuckle

Cute Blue Shuckle

Note to parents:
Pokémon names can be hard to pronounce!
Please use this guide to help your child sound
out the names included in this book:

Shuckle: SHUCK-kull

Bellsprout: BELL-sprout

by Quinlan B. Lee

© 2018 The Pokémon Company International. © 1997–2018 Nintendo, Creatures, GAME FREAK, TV Tokyo, ShoPro, JR Kikaku. TM, ® Nintendo.

Published by Scholastic Inc., *Publishers since 1920.* SCHOLASTIC and associated logos are trademarks and/or registered trademarks of Scholastic Inc.

Scholastic Inc., 557 Broadway, New York, NY 10012

978-1-338-23129-8

10 9 8 7 6 5 4   21 22 23 24 25

Printed in Rawang, Malaysia   106
First printing 2018

SCHOLASTIC INC.

This is a **blue** Shuckle.
It is **cute**.
Blue Shuckle **juice** is cool.
It makes Pokémon fall in love.

An old man knows about **blue**
Shuckle.
"We need a **clue**," Brock says.

"Where can we find a **blue** Shuckle?" Brock asks.
They **use** the old man's Bellsprout.

Bellsprout finds the **cute blue** Shuckle.

Oh no.
Team Rocket finds the **blue**
Shuckle, too!

Jessie drinks **blue** Shuckle **juice**.

The **blue juice** makes lots of Pokémon come to Jessie. They are in love with her!

The old man's words were **true**.
The **blue juice** made Shuckle
fall in love.

Help!
Jessie does not have a **clue**.
What should she do?

The old man has a **clue**.
He **uses** magic powder.

Now the Pokémon are
not in love with Jessie.

"Want to **use** the **blue** Shuckle **juice**?" the old man asks Brock.

"No," Brock says.
"Pokémon should like me for me.
Not for some **blue juice**!"

Blue Shuckle **juice** is cool.
It makes Pokémon fall in love.
Now Pokémon love Jessie!
What should she do?

In this book, you will practice these **long U** words:

blue	clue	cute
juice	true	use

978-1-338-23129-8

scholastic.com

PHONICS

Book 12
Long Vowel
Review

So Much to See

So Much to See

Note to parents:

Pokémon names can be hard to pronounce!
Please use this guide to help your child sound
out the names included in this book:

Grubbin: GRUB-bin

Bewear: beh-WARE

Pikachu: PEE-ka-choo

Tauros: TORE-ros

by Quinlan B. Lee

Published by Scholastic Inc., *Publishers since 1920.* SCHOLASTIC and associated logos are trademarks
and/or registered trademarks of Scholastic Inc.

The publisher does not have any control over and does not assume any responsibility for
author or third-party websites or their content.

This book is a work of fiction. Names, characters, places, and incidents are either the product of the author's imagination
or are used fictitiously, and any resemblance to actual persons, living or dead, business establishments,
events, or locales is entirely coincidental.

Scholastic Inc., 557 Broadway, New York, NY 10012

978-1-338-23130-4

10 9 8 7 6 5 4   21 22 23 24 25

Printed in Rawang, Malaysia   106
First printing 2018

SCHOLASTIC INC.

Alola is cool!

The **sky** is **blue**.
The **sea** is **blue**.

There are cool **places** to go.
Ash **rides** the **waves**.
He dives in the **sea**.

Ash **sees** a Grubbin.
It looks **nice**.

It gets Ash's **nose**.
Ow!
Then it runs **away**.

"Let's **race** it!" Ash says.
Grubbin **hides** in the woods.

There are so many **trees**.
They can not **see** Grubbin.
Ash does not have a **clue**.

They **see** a Pokémon.
It is Bewear!
It swings at a **tree**.

Bewear **chases** them.
It is **huge**!
Ash and Pikachu run **away**.

Ash and Pikachu run into
Mallow.
She rides a Tauros.

Mallow takes them to
Pokémon School.
"School is a cool **place**!"
says Ash.

Ash and Pikachu **meet**
new Pokémon.
They are cool!

Ash does not want to **leave** Alola.
There is so much to **see**.
He and Pikachu **stay**.

Ash and Pikachu are in Alola.
There is so much to **see**!

In this book, you will practice these **long vowel** words:

away	blue	chase
clue	dive	he
hide	huge	leave
meet	nice	nose
place	race	ride
sea	see	she
sky	stay	tree
wave		

978-1-338-23130-4